Hansel and Gretel

Scholastic Children's Books,
Commonwealth House, 1 – 19 New Oxford Street, London WC1A 1NU
A division of Scholastic Limited
London – New York – Toronto – Sydney – Auckland

Published by Scholastic Limited 1996
Copyright © Carlton UK Television Limited MCMXCVI

A Traditional tale adapted by Ed Welch
Designed by Sara and Simon Bor
Based on the series Wolves, Witches and Giants
A Wolf Gang Cartoons production by Honeycomb Animation for
Carlton UK Television

ISBN 0 590 13716 6

Printed and bound in Italy by Amadeus

10 9 8 7 6 5 4 3 2 1

The right of Ed Welch and Sara and Simon Bor to be identified as the
author/adaptor and designers of this work respectively has been asserted by
them in accordance with the Copyright, Designs and Patents Act, 1988.

Once upon a time, by a great forest, there lived a poor woodcutter and his wife with their two children, a boy called Hansel and a girl called Gretel.

"Oh, what are we going to do? We haven't enough bread to feed ourselves, let alone the children."

"Simple," said his cruel wife. "We'll set off tomorrow with the children deep into the woods, and leave them there. They'll never find their way back, and we'll be rid of them forever."

The woodcutter was horrified at his wife's plan, as were poor Hansel and Gretel.

Poor Gretel started to cry her eyes out.
"Oh, quiet. I'll think of a way out of this," said Hansel.

Outside the cottage, Hansel filled his pockets to bursting with shiny pebbles and crept back inside and up to bed.

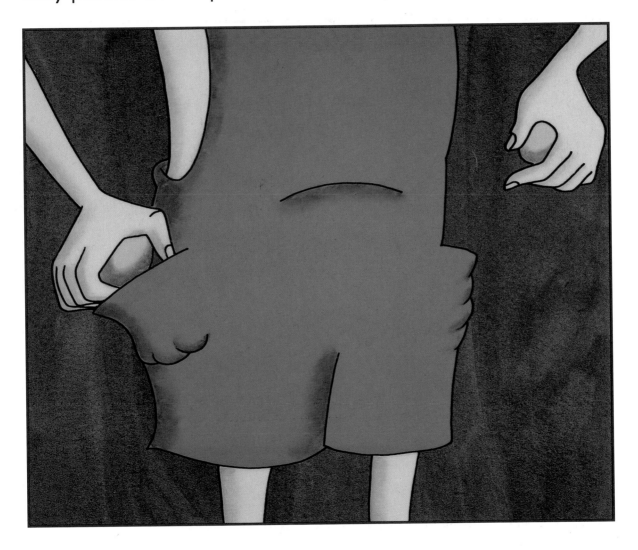

At dawn, their mother shook the children roughly to wake them. "Get up, you lazybones! We're off to collect wood."

She gave them each a little piece of bread and off the family went, Hansel's pockets bulging with the pebbles.

Unknown to his parents, Hansel dropped a shiny pebble every so often, until they arrived in the middle of the forest.

Their father built a fire for them and told the children to wait by it until they returned.
"You will hear us chopping wood nearby, so don't be frightened."

But of course, they were, especially in case there were any wolves about.

All day the children waited, listening to the sound of an axe, but, in fact, the cruel mother had tied a log to a tree trunk and left it flapping in the wind.

"This is gonna take some thought."

It was quite dark by now and Gretel began to cry again.

"Oh, SHUT UP!" said Hansel, telling her to wait till the moon rose, then they would find their way home.

Sure enough, when the moon had risen, all the little pebbles Hansel had dropped shone on the path like new silver coins. They followed them back and arrived home in time for a wholesome breakfast of stale bread and water.

"You naughty children. We thought the Wolf might have got you."

Later that evening, the children heard their parents having their traditional evening row.

"This time, we shall take them even further into the forest."

When she heard this, Gretel cried her eyes out, then back in again.

"Don't worry. I'll think of something, said Hansel." He thought of elephants, but it wasn't any use.

The next morning, the family set off again into the woods. Hansel trailed behind, dropping little morsels of bread he had crumbled up, as he had dropped pebbles a day earlier.

This time the children were led even deeper into the woods, and as before, their parents left them by a little fire.

When they had gone, Hansel reassured his sister they would be able to follow the trail of breadcrumbs in the moonlight, just like the shiny pebbles.

But whereas birds and mice do not eat
pebbles, they do eat inviting little morsels
of bread (and an occasional elephant), so
when the moon rose, Hansel found that his
trail of breadcrumbs was gone, and the children
were lost in the middle of a huge, dark forest.

Quite suddenly, they came across a little cottage made of gingerbread, with a roof of chocolate biscuits and windows of barley sugar. The children, who were starving anyway, set to work breaking off bits of house and eating away to their heart's content.

Suddenly, the door was opened - by a WITCH!

"You must be very tired. Why don't you have a cup of hot chocolate?"

"Another two for the pot. When I've fattened them up, they'll make a wonderful meal. Ah, ha, ha, ha!"

The Witch enticed children to her cottage because it was made of chocolate and sugar.
She grabbed Hansel and put a spell on him. . .

"Cauliflower, pastry, treacle and jam,
The wickedest witch in the world's who I am!"

In a flash, Hansel was trapped in a cage.

"Go and cook something for your brother. When he is fat enough, I'll eat him up. Ah, ha, ha, ha!"

Every morning, the Witch went to the grille of Hansel's cage.

"Hansel, stretch out your finger so I can
feel if you are fat enough to eat."

But Hansel, a clever boy, with two 'A' levels, pushed through a thin
bone he had found in the bottom of his cage, and the Witch, (who
had poor eyesight, no 'A' levels and a poor sense of humour) was
astonished at how long it was taking to fatten him up.

"I can't wait any longer," she said. "Go and fill the cauldron with water, girl. Today, fat or thin, I shall eat him up. Aha, ha, ha!"

The Witch started to prepare some dough for baking.

"I shall need some fresh bread with my supper, hee, hee, hee! Gretel, open the oven door to see if it's hot enough for baking. (When she's in there, I'll slam the door, and eat her as well!)"

Gretel knew what was on the Witch's mind (it looked like hair), so she asked the Witch to show her how to open the oven door.

"Stupid child!" screamed the Witch. "Let me show you!" The Witch opened the door, and with an almightly shove, Gretel pushed the Witch in and slammed the door.

"YEOW!"

Gretel rushed to release Hansel, and they eventually found themselves back at their cottage.

They were not sorry to learn that their cruel mother had left their father to join the army, and the children lived with their father happily ever after.